Published by Modern Publishing. A Division of Unisystems, Inc.
My Modern World of Words™ is a trademark owned by Joshua Morris Publishing Inc.
Copyright © 1987 by Joshua Morris Publishing Inc. All rights reserved.
Printed in Belgium

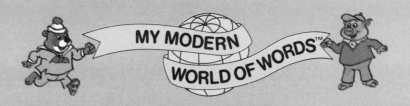

MY MODERN
WORLD OF WORDS™

Race Around the World

Written and Illustrated by

David Gantz

Modern Publishing
A Division of Unisystems, Inc.
New York, New York 10022

The big race around the world is about to begin.
Oscar Dog and his friends Willy Bear and Roz
and Ralph O'Hare will travel over and across
many countries by air, land and sea.

"Good luck, Oscar!" shouts Willy, as he flaps his
motor wings.
"See you at the finish line, Willy!" says Oscar,
starting up his trusty airplane.
"I can't wait to see the rest of the world!"
exclaims Roz.

Down goes the starting flag. They're off!
"Look out world—here we come!" cries Ralph as
their hot air balloon sails into the air.

Willy takes the lead early, just as they fly over New York Harbor. Roz looks back at all the tall buildings, but the most amazing sight she sees is the Statue of Liberty!

Empire State Building

Chrysler Building

skyscrapers

World Trade Center

BARBARA + LARRY

tug boat

barge

Statue of Liberty

ferry

Liberty Island

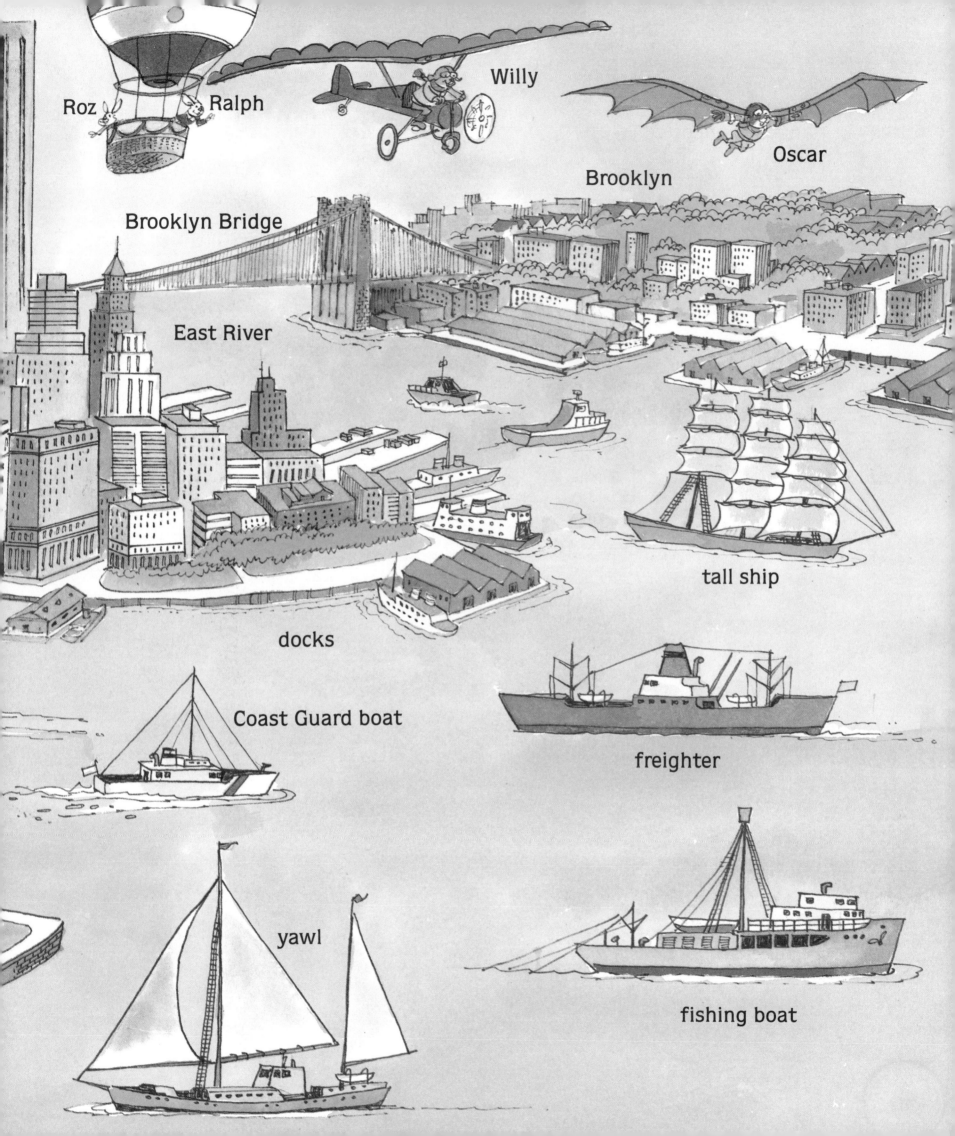

Roz

Ralph

Willy

Oscar

Brooklyn

Brooklyn Bridge

East River

tall ship

docks

Coast Guard boat

freighter

yawl

fishing boat

Next, the racers fly over Ottawa, Canada just in time to see the Canadian mounted police patrol the House of Parliament.

snow geese

Canada's flag

Oscar

Ralph

Roz

Willy

House of Parliament

mounted policemen

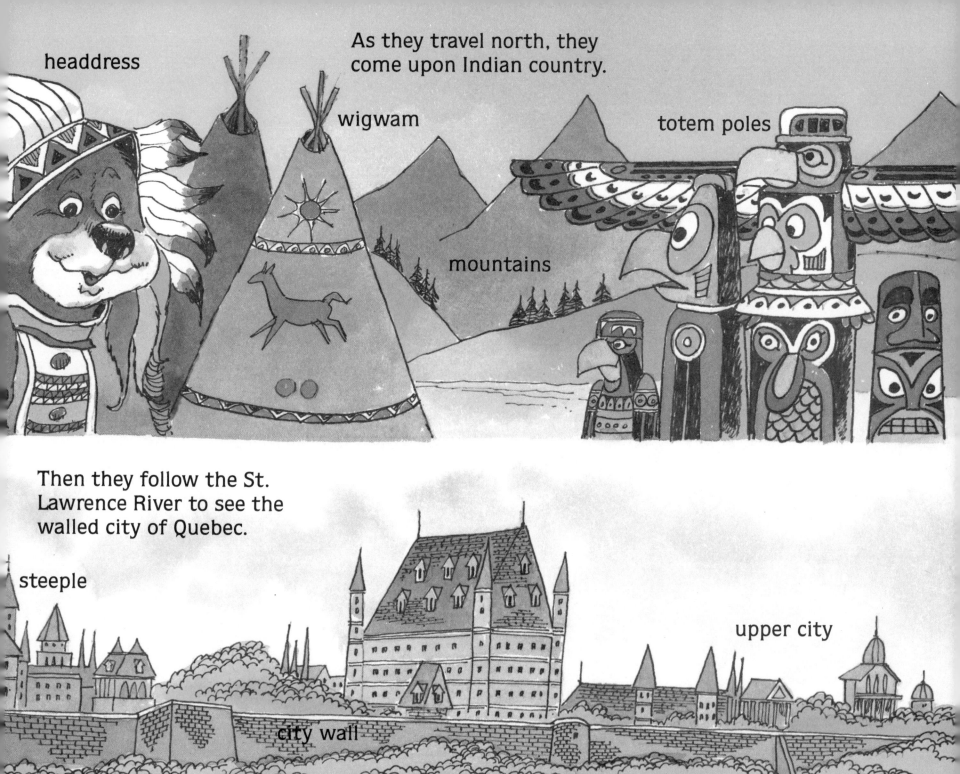

headdress

As they travel north, they come upon Indian country.

wigwam

totem poles

mountains

Then they follow the St. Lawrence River to see the walled city of Quebec.

steeple

upper city

city wall

lower city

St. Lawrence River

In London, England, the four friends take time out from the race to jog across the Tower Bridge.

Thames River

Tower Bridge

tug boat

double decker bus

guard house

They stop to get a closer look at the Beefeaters, who guard the Tower of London.

Beefeater guards

Ralph

Roz

Queen's guard

Willy

Osc

As they rent bicy-
cles and speed past
Big Ben, Ralph
shoots out in front.
The race is on
again!

Houses of Parliament

skates

bicycle

scooter

Tower of London

Willy pulls out in front as the race moves to Scandinavia, where the racers zip over the icy snow in sleighs pulled by reindeer!

Oscar

a Lapp home

log hauling horse sleigh

Roz and Ralph

a Lapp family

herd of reindeer

snowshoes

reindeer sleigh

Willy

stave church

troll

gnome

They heard thrilling fairy tales about trolls and gnomes.

Scandinavian women in traditional clothing

But in Norway, they race past an old
fishing village in Viking ships!

fishing village

a fjord

Roz and Ralph's ship

Willy's ship

fishing boats

figurehead

Oscar's ship

viking ships

Swedish Castle Kalmar

The race gets going in Holland as the friends
float past windmills and paddle through a
village canal.

North Sea

flour mill

waterwheel

bridge

canal barge

Roz and Ralph

tub

Oscar

canal

raft

windmills

train

dock

Willy

innertube

The racers are back in the air as they fly over West Germany. However, Roz and Ralph's balloon gets caught on a castle tower.

Roz and Ralph

Willy

While the balloon is being repaired they all do some sightseeing.

Oscar

clock tower

Tower

mountains

King Ludwig the Second's Fairytale Castle

lamp

archway

They visit the medieval town of Rothenburg.

forest

storks

storks' nest

In an old Bavarian town, they watch a brass band parade by.

balcony

bugle

trombone

ivy

drum

trumpet

tuba

German brass band

water fountain

dachshund

When they got to Paris, France, Oscar, Ralph, Roz, and Willy stopped the race to climb to the top of the Eiffel Tower.

Roz, Ralph, Oscar and Willy

hot air balloons

blimp

Eiffel Tower

townhouses

artist's studio

awning

poster kiosk

GALERIE PHARMACIE

Later, they jogged for fun through the Arc 'd Triomphe.

Then they started up the race again in boats down the River Seine.

GRANDMA + GRANDPA INSIDE

River Seine

Cathedral of Notre Dame

painting

rowboat

artist

picnickers

paddle boat

motor boat

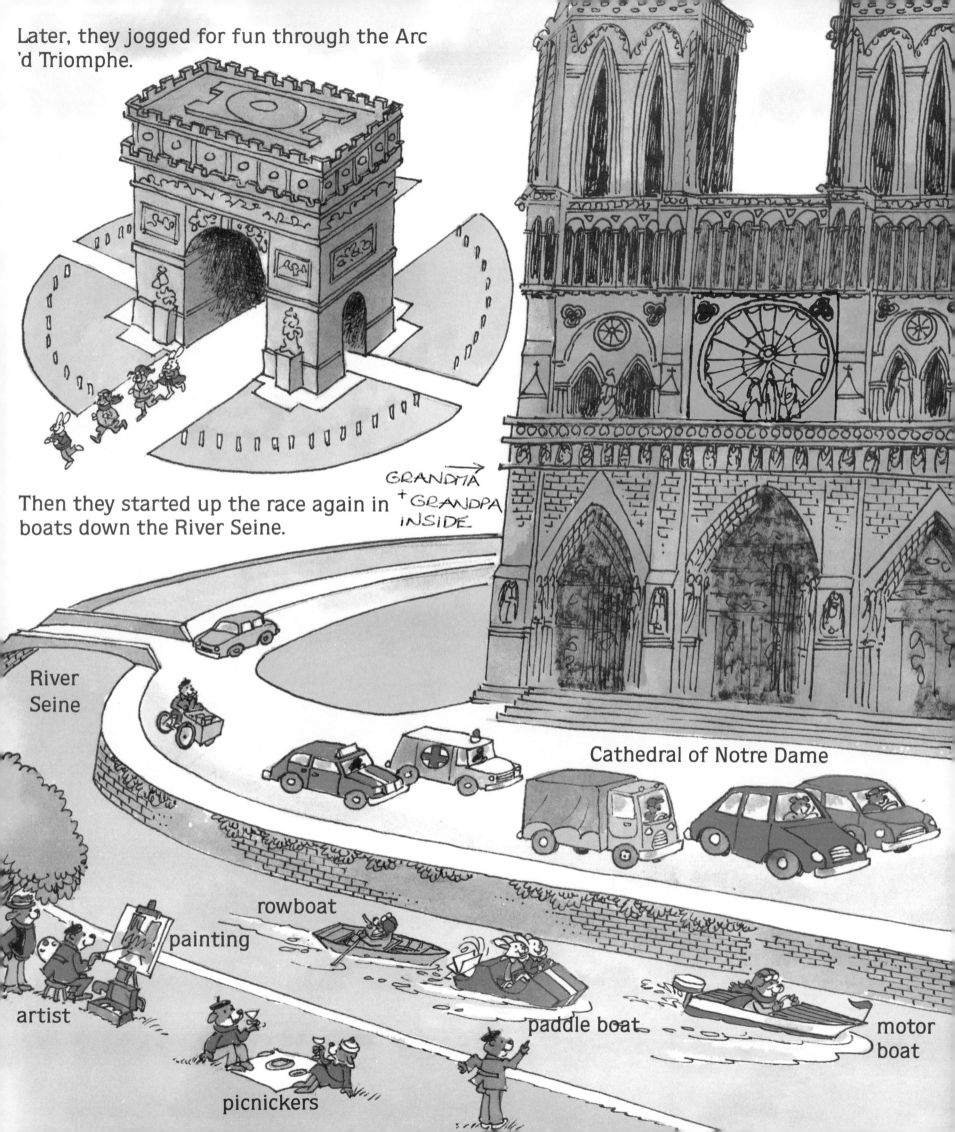

Ralph

Roz

Oscar

Willy

They fly on to Switzerland, where the race continues as they ski down a mountain with Willy in the lead.

castle

mountain goats

wall clock

cuckcoo clock

mantel clock

Lake Geneva

The Matterhorn

The Alps

Swiss Flag

pasture

chalet

walking stick

firewood

dirndl dress

Swiss cheese

alphorn

In Italy, the racers fly over many farms and orchards.

olive orchard

sheep

cows

haystack

blacksmith's shop

water well

church processional

corn bin

Roz and Ralph's balloon leads as they pass the city of Pisa.

Leaning Tower of Pisa

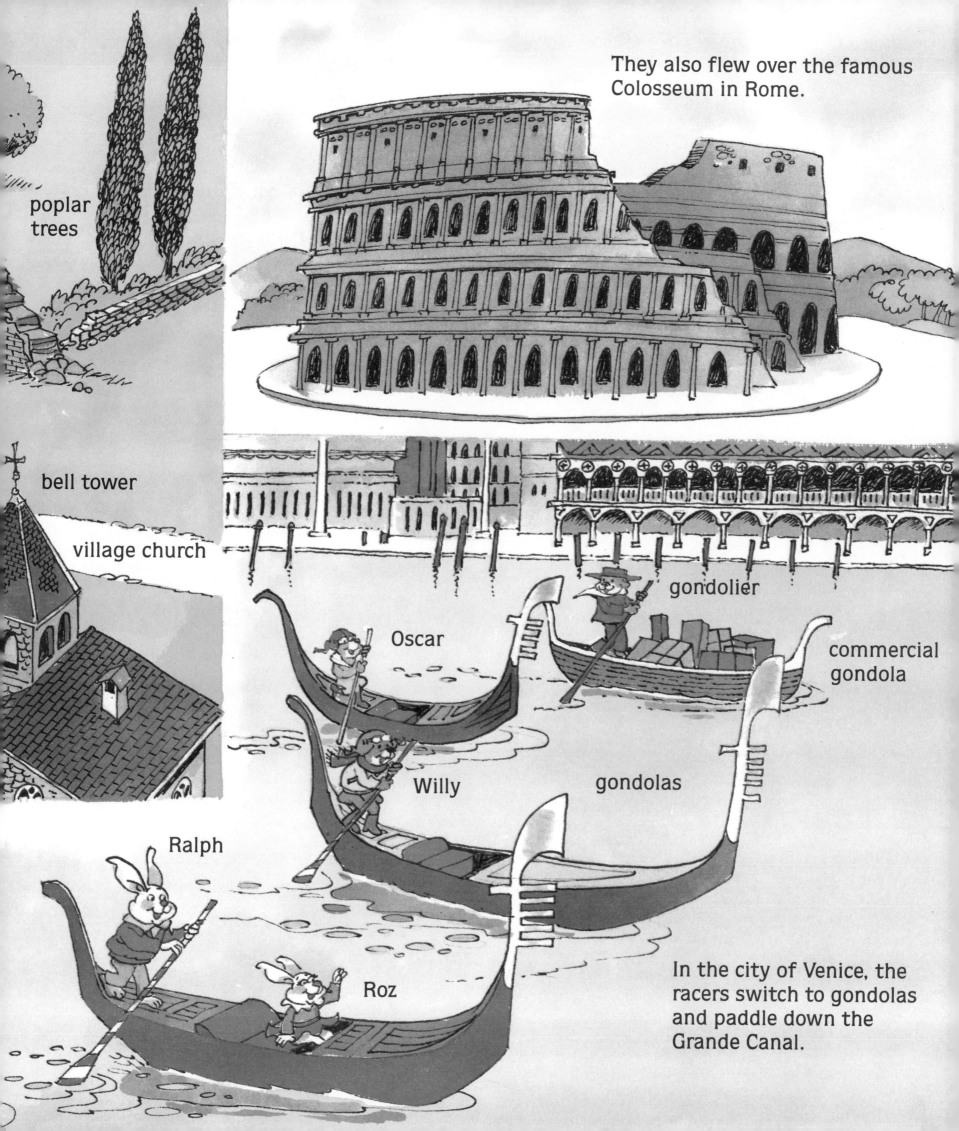

poplar trees

They also flew over the famous Colosseum in Rome.

bell tower

village church

Oscar

gondolier

commercial gondola

Willy

gondolas

Ralph

Roz

In the city of Venice, the racers switch to gondolas and paddle down the Grande Canal.

Willy

Roz

Ralph

Oscar

The racers are neck and neck in Spain as they fly over the castle where King Ferdinand and Queen Isabella once lived.

castle

turrets

plateau

poplar trees

tourists

hanging houses

terraced farm fields

battlement

shepherd

pasture

bull

matador

cape

bull ring

They then take a break to see a
bullfight and shop in a Spanish marketplace.

aqueduct

windmills

mandolin

priest

donkey cart

milkman

The race continues in Egypt as they bounce through the desert on camels, past pyramids and ancient ruins.

minaret

pyramids

mosque

Sphinx

Oscar

ancient ruins

Willy

Ralph

desert

camel

Later, they stop to visit a marketplace in a little town near Cairo.

Roz

bananas

oranges

pots

bread

corn

donkey

rice sacks

bicycle

ox

chimpanzees

Ralph

Roz

drums

log butter churn

Oscar

pelican

elephant

crocodile

In India, they're flying again—over the famous cave temple of Ajanta.

cave temple

sari

city wall

Oscar

Then the four friends take another break to ride in bicycle taxis past an outdoor market.

maharajah

maharani

elephant

Ralph

Roz

bicycle taxis

Willy

peddler

rope climber

magician

dome

Taj Mahal

Roz thinks that the Taj Mahal is the prettiest building she's ever seen.

rope

cobra

basket

pagoda

In China, the race moves on as rickshaws bounce Willy, Oscar, Roz, and Ralph for miles and miles along the Great Wall.

terraced fields

Willy

Oscar

Roz and Ralph

jugglers

rickshaw

acrobats

dragon kite

shrine

toll booth

village

oxcart

dock

water
carriers

pandas

As Roz, Ralph, Oscar, and Willy approach Japan, they fly over Mount Fuji.

Roz and Ralph

Oscar

Willy

Mount Fuji

farm houses

rice planters

rice paddies

bonsai tree

long tail fowl

kimono

sumo wrestlers

Later, they pass a Buddhist shrine.

Buddha

temple

incense burner

referee

carp wind sock

caligrapher

The race is even as they fly over Sydney Harbor in Australia.

Roz

Ralph

Oscar

Willy

Australian flag

Sydney Harbor Bridge

Sydney Opera House

Sydney Harbor

Australian coat of arms

AUSTRALIA

ferry

doc

The four friends stop the race so they can visit the Australian outback.

boomerangs

aborigine shield

dingo dogs

baobob trees

wallaby

cassowary

kangaroos

koala

Australian lizard

kookaburra

platypus

In Mexico, they take time out from the race to visit a street fair in a little village.

piñata

Roz

Ralph

cathedral

violinist

trumpeter

guitarist

tortillas

chile peppers

Mariachi band

ancient Aztec ruins

jungle

Oscar

balloon vendor

firewood

Willy

chickens

goats

dancers

pottery

The race takes off again, as they fly through the sky over Rio de Janeiro in Brazil. Roz and Ralph wave to the pilot of a nearby helicopter.

Oscar

Willy

Roz and Ralph

helicopter

Sugarloaf Mountain

harbor

Later, they take a sightseeing ride down the great Amazon River.

shaggy anteater

Rio de Janeiro Bay

beach

tourists

jungle

Indian village

river boat

toucan

Amazon River

macaws

flamingos

armadillo

banner

WELCOME HOME

Ralph   Roz

trophy

mayor   Will

At the finish line, Roz, Ralph, Willy and Oscar find the biggest surprise of all—they arrive at the same time!

"It's a tie!" shouts the crowd.
"But there is only one prize," says the mayor.
"That's okay," chime Roz and Ralph.
"We're all winners!" says Willy.
"And our wonderful trip around the world was the best prize of all!" says Oscar.

balloons

Oscar

finish line